Harry
and
LuLu

Arthur Yorinks

Illustrated by Martin Matje

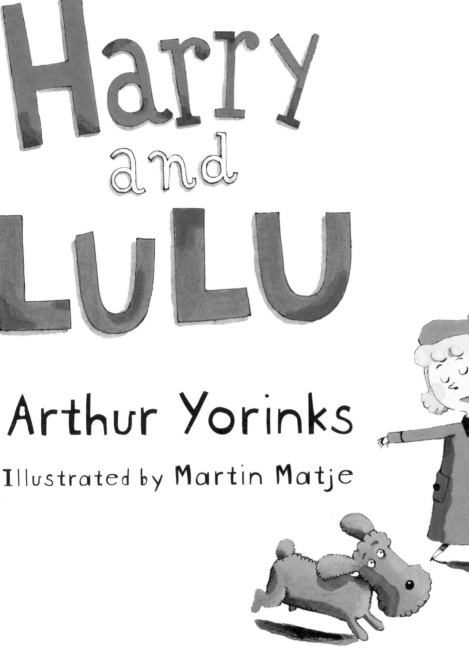

Hyperion Books for Children
New York

For Harry, Irma, Lulu, and Adrienne
—A. Y.

First Edition
1 3 5 7 9 10 8 6 4 2

The artwork for this book was prepared in watercolor and gouache.
Printed in Singapore.
This book is set in 20-point Bernhard Modern

Library of Congress Cataloging-in-Publication Data
Yorinks, Arthur.
Harry and Lulu / Arthur Yorinks: illustrated by Martin Matje.
p. cm.
Summary: Lulu, who has always wanted a dog, instead gets a very unusual stuffed ani-
mal that takes her on a trip to France.
ISBN 0-7868-0335-5 (trade)— ISBN 0-7868-2276-7 (library)
[1. Dogs-Fiction. 2. Toys—Fiction. 3. Paris (France)—Fiction. 4. France—Fiction.]
I. Matje, Martin, ill. II. Title.
PZ7.Y819Har 1999
[E]-dc21 97-28205

Her parents weren't altogether bad. When little
Lulu asked for the fortieth time, "Please can I
have a dog?" and they answered loudly, "NO!"
they did give her Harry, a stuffed toy red poodle.

But Lulu went lulu.

I WANT
a REAL
DOG!

"I want a real dog! I WANT A REAL DOG!" she yelled. And she threw poor stuffed Harry onto the floor and kicked him and stamped her feet and banged the wall and slammed her door. Whew!

Well, all children, even wild maniac children,
deserve a wish now and then. Or at least half a wish.
And one night, Lulu got hers.

It was Thursday. At nine. Lulu
was supposed to be asleep by eight
but she read five comic books and
one spooky chapter of a mystery
book before she finally fell asleep.

That's when Harry, the toy
poodle, barked.

"Woof! Woof!"

Okay, it was kind of a squeaky
bark, but it was a bark all right.
Lulu woke up with a start.

"Harry?" she said, looking at Harry.

Harry jumped up on the bed and licked Lulu's face from top to bottom. Lulu was delirious. Then she remembered.

"Wait a minute," she said to Harry. "You're not a dog. You're just a stupid stuffed animal and maybe I should throw you out the window or kick you down the sewer or something!" Lulu went to grab him.

Harry thought of yelping for help, but instead he decided to speak English.

"Lulu," he said. "You should *never* kick a dog!"

Harry gave a wiggle as if his side hurt. What an actor.

"But, you're a toy!" Lulu defended herself.

"You shouldn't even THINK about kicking a dog!"
Harry stood his ground.

"ALL RIGHT ALREADY!" Lulu shouted.

"I'm . . . sorry," she whispered.

Holy moly. An apology? That was a first.
And though it would have been nice to stop
right there, Lulu didn't. She didn't skip a beat.
   "You're still a toy," she declared. "And I'll
prove it." Lulu put on her slippers. "Follow me!"
   Harry followed Lulu out the door and down
the stairs to the kitchen.

On the counter, Lulu found the canister filled with dog biscuits she made her mother buy in anticipation of—well, you know—and offered one to Harry.

"Here, let's see you eat one of these," she dared.

"Yucch!" Harry thought to himself. "I'm not eating a dog biscuit."

"I knew it," Lulu said. "I knew it." Lulu's eyes got all watery. "You're no dog," she said, determined with all her might not to cry.

Lulu put away the biscuits and tried to cheer herself up with a pumpernickel bagel. That usually worked. But Harry went nuts.

"I love bagels!" he said. He spun around, jumped, and snatched Lulu's bagel right out of her hand. "Hey!" she shouted.

Harry was in heaven. As he chewed with gusto, Lulu sighed.

"I guess I'll never have a dog," she said.

"But I'm a dog," said Harry with his mouth full.

"You are not, you are not, you are NOT!" yelled
Lulu.

"I am too, I am too, I am TOO!" growled Harry.
"And maybe I'll pack up and go back to where I
came from."

"Oh, yeah?" Lulu smirked. "Where's that? Abe's
Toy Store?"

"France," said Harry.

"France!" Lulu piped up. "I don't believe you."

"See if I care," Harry replied. "I'm leaving!"

At that, Lulu thought and said, "Well, maybe I'll go with you." And Harry said, "Why don't you, big shot." And Lulu said, "Okay, I will." And Harry said, "Good!"

So Harry and Lulu, both still steaming, started to walk toward the back door when suddenly Lulu stopped and exclaimed, "I can't go like this! Not in pajamas! Wait here and don't move."

Lulu scurried up to her bedroom where she put
on one outfit, then another outfit, then still
another outfit until she had tried on every outfit
she owned and decided the first one was best. It
did look very nice. She had a hat and everything.
Then she ran back downstairs to the kitchen
where Harry was waiting like a gentleman.

Lulu opened the back door and they both went outside.

"Isn't it far to France?" Lulu asked as they walked down the block.

"It only seems that way when you're traveling at night," explained Harry. He really didn't know what he was talking about but it didn't matter to Lulu and it didn't matter to Harry either. They were having a great time walking together.

Such a great time, in fact, that before they knew it, it was morning and they had arrived in Paris.

"Oh, it's beautiful," exclaimed Lulu.

"Yes, it is," said Harry as they stopped to take in the view.

They stood on a wide boulevard
that had a name neither of them
could pronounce. There was the
Eiffel Tower. There was the Louvre.
There was Notre Dame.

Still, even in Paris, Lulu
was Lulu.

"Now go away and do something," she said to Harry. "I don't want people to think I'm hanging around with a stuffed animal."

Harry looked up at Lulu with his dog brown eyes. Even if Lulu didn't know it yet, he was a dog, her dog, and like all dogs, he had a heart as big as the moon or Jupiter. And though she could say and do all the mean things in the world to him, he still loved her and was loyal to her and, so as not to embarrass her, he walked around pretending not to know her but never once took his eyes off her.

It was a lucky thing, too. Because Lulu,
who first sat at an outdoor café and had a hot
chocolate (very Parisian) and then strolled
around and looked at the buildings and the
sculptures and the people going by, didn't look
where she was going.

A car, speeding, and bleeping its French
horn all the way, had turned the corner and
was headed right for Lulu!

Harry ran. He ran, and he ran, and he ran, and he ran, and he jumped into the air and nudged Lulu out of harm's way. But he went sailing straight into the rushing river Seine.

"There's a dog in the river!" a bystander called
out. "There's a dog in the river!"

A crowd gathered. Lulu stopped. She looked.
She was about to yell, "That's not a dog, it's just a
stuffed animal," but she couldn't get out the words.
She saw Harry's head bobbing up and down in
the water and when she heard his squeaky voice
say, "Lulu, help!" first her heart raced and then
her legs raced and suddenly she cried out,
"That's MY dog!"

She jumped into the water and scooped Harry up and carried him to safety. Lulu was a very good swimmer.

"Harry!" Lulu cried. She hugged him with his scrappy short front legs wrapped around her neck. "Oh, Harry!" she said and gave him a big, fat kiss.

Filled with dog love, Lulu thought of nothing else and, in no time, she and Harry were back from France, back upstairs in her bedroom, in her bed, safe, warm, and dry.

As their eyes closed, Lulu asked, "You're not really from France, are you?"

"No," Harry murmured. "Indiana." And they were both fast asleep.

Lulu's parents, the kind that get up very early in the
morning, got up early the next day and looked in on Lulu.
"Look," her mother said to her father. "She loves the toy."
Little did they know.